The Witch Sisters of Dublin Louisiana

Michele Linn Griffith

God Is My Rock!

ABOUT THE AUTHOR!

Michele Linn Griffith is a fictional writer who is an avid reader. She is a native of Alabama.

mgriffith75@yahoo.com

Philippians 4:13

This story is the product of the authors imagination, and all naming of characters places, incidents and businesses are all fictitious.

Dublin Louisiana is a small town, with the population less then twenty thousand. It's home to the Witch covens. They've been there for centuries.

The Witch Covens have managed to fly under the radar and live normal lives amongst the Humans, without them suspecting anything.

CHAPTER 1

Lucinda Dorinda, Elenore and Celeste Lamberson are sisters who are known as the Witch sisters of Dublin.

CHAPTER 2

Lucinda and Dorinda are thirty years old, and they are twins who are the oldest of the four. They were born on October thirty first of nineteen eighty eight, which was on Halloween to the parents of Patricia and Randall.

Both ladies are wives, mothers and they are the owners of a unique Boutique called Spellbound.

CHAPTER 3

Elenore is the third child out of four and she is twenty eight years old.

She was born on November twenty fourth of nineteen ninety, which just happens to be on Thanksgiving.

She owns her own her own flower shop.

She is pregnant with her first child. Although the father isn't in the picture.

CHAPTER 4

Celeste is the youngest of the four. She is twenty six years old.

She was born on December twenty fifth nineteen ninety two, which was just happens to be on Christmas Day.

She co-owns a bakery called C&J's Sweet Treats with her best friend Jennabe.

She is a single lady who is perfectly happy on her own.

CHAPTER 5

Patricia and Randall have been married thirty years.

They've been together since they were in kindergarten.

They married when they were seventeen and soon after they gave birth to twin daughters.

Their life together has been great but

not easy.

Patricia owns her own décor boutique and has for a very long time. In fact, she's had her business since her early twenties.

Randall owns his own construction business which he's had since his early twenties.

CHAPTER 6

It's Friday morning around six a.m. and Lucinda was in her kitchen brewing coffee and making breakfast when she heard the front door open and then close.

Within minutes her husband Devin walked into the kitchen, "hey babe," said Devin.

Lucinda turned around saying, "oh, hey honey," said Lucinda. "How was work?"

"Busy," said Devin. "Crazy busy." "Oh

wow, I'm sorry to hear that," said Lucinda.

"Oh, it's okay it's part of being a police officer," said Devin.

Lucinda smiled, "yeah, I guess it is," said Lucinda.

Devin smiled. "Well now, babe how was your night?" asked Devin.

"Well like you busy, the girls Alex and Alisa are keeping me busy," said Lucinda. "Oh yeah, by the way, are you off this weekend?"

"Yes." "Why?" asked Devin curiously. "Well, I could use your help this weekend," said Lucinda.

"Yeah sure, count me in," said Devin. "So, what do you have in mind?"

"Well honey, we are hosting a fall festival which starts tonight and so I thought maybe you could help us setup," said Lucinda.

"Okay." "Yeah sure," said Devin. "So, who's we anyway?"

"Well, me and our girls Alex and Alisa and Dorinda and her girls Chris and Chasity," said Lucinda.

"Oh, okay," said Devin. "So, why aren't the girls going to school today?" asked Devin.

"The school is closed today due to a teacher workday," said Lucinda.

"Oh, okay," said Devin. "Well, when is Dorinda and the girls coming?"

"Anytime," said Lucinda. "Great." "Well let me get a nap and then I'll be glad to help," said Devin.

"Alright." "Well, while you're taking a nap, I'm going to start working on decorating the house and yard, but first I'm going to drink my coffee and breakfast," said Lucinda.

"Okay." "Well, I'll help you when I get up," said Devin, and then he started walking towards the stairs.

A few minutes later their daughters Alex and Alisa came walking down the stairs and soon after they were walking into the kitchen, "hey mom," said Alex and Alisa.

She turned around, "oh good morning girls," said Lucinda. "Well come on let's eat some breakfast and let's get started on the busy day of decorating."

"Okay." "Yes ma'am," said Alex and Alisa, and then they sat down at the kitchen table and started eating.

CHAPTER 7

Thirty minutes later Lucinda and her girls were finished eating breakfast and were finishing up with the kitchen cleanup.

"Hey mom," said Alex. "Yes Alex," said Lucinda.

"Mom, we were wondering, what time is this fall festival thing tonight?" asked Alex.

"Oh, I'm thinking maybe six," said Lucinda. "Why you asking anyway?"

"Well mom our friends were asking," said Alex.

"Oh okay, that's cool," said Lucinda. "Well come on let's get started with the cleaning and decorating."

"Okay." "Yes ma'am," said Alex and Alisa, and then they hurried off in the direction of the stairs.

When they were out of sight, she just shook her head and laughed. Her twelve year old twin girls never ceases to amaze her.

She was busy working on her chore of

cleaning and decorating, when she heard the door open up and her twin sister call out, "Luc we're here," said Dorinda.

She rounded the corner finding Lucinda dusting and decorating the den, "hi sis," said Dorinda.

Lucinda turned around, "oh hey sis and girls," said Lucinda. "Thank you for coming to help."

"Yeah sure, why wouldn't we?" said Dorinda. "Well now, where do you want us to start?"

"Well, you can help me in here," said Lucinda.

"Okay." "Well let's get started," said Dorinda, and so she and the girls got to work.

CHAPTER 8

It was around noonish, when Lucinda, Dorinda and their four girls walked into the kitchen and sat down to lunch, "wow we got a lot done in a short time," said Lucinda.

"Yeah, we did," said Dorinda. "Well now, what's next?"

"Oh, we have a lot more to get done before tonight," said Lucinda.

"Alright then." "Well let's get to it," said Dorinda.

"Yeah let's," said Lucinda. Suddenly she heard footsteps coming down the steps, and soon after her husband Devin walked into the kitchen, "hey honey," said Lucinda.

"Hey babe," said Devin. "Well, did you sleep good?" Lucinda asked.

"Yeah, I did," said Devin. "Good, I'm glad" said Lucinda.

"So babe, where do you want me to start?"

"Outside would be a great place to start honey," said Lucinda.

"Okay." "Well, I'm on it," said Devin. "Thank you, babe," said Lucinda.

"Yeah sure, you're welcome, and I wouldn't have it any other way," said Devin.

Lucinda smiled, "thank you honey for all that you do for me and our girls," said Lucinda happily.

"Aww, honey you're welcome," said Devin, and then he headed out the door.

CHAPTER 9

Around three thirty p.m. Lucinda and Devin's house and yard were decorated fully with everything Halloween.

"Omg, this looks so amazing, you guys did so good," said Lucinda squealed. "Devin, Dorinda and girls you guys did an awesome job."

"Thank you." "We aim to please and we're so glad we can be apart of this," said Dorinda and the girls.

"Honey, I wouldn't have any other way, I love that we celebrate every kinda holiday fully," said Devin.

"Me too," said Lucinda. "Well come on let's go get ready for this Halloween Fall Festival."

CHAPTER 10

Around five p.m. Celeste and Jennabe pulled up in front of her big sister's house, "oh wow this looks amazing," said Jennabe.

"Yeah, it does, but my big sister goes above and beyond when it comes to any Holiday," said Celeste.

Jennabe smiled, "yeah no doubt," said

Jennabe.

"Well come on let's get this food inside," said Celeste, and so they exited the van, and walked around to the back, and opened up the doors, and started unloading the van of foods and pastries onto a large pushcart.

Within minutes they had the pushcart loaded down, and afterwards they were heading towards the front door.

As they were walking up to the door, the door flew open and there standing was Alex, "hey Alex," said Celeste.

"Hey Auntie C, and Ms. Jannabe," said Alex. "Come on in."

"Thanks," said Celeste and Jannabe, and so they started pushing the pushcart through the door.

As they were walking through the house pushing the pushcart, they were met by Devin, "hey Celeste and Jannabe, I'm so glad you could come and provide us the food and treats for this Halloween party," said Devin.

"Yeah sure, no problem," said Celeste. "Although we wouldn't have any other way."

Devin smiled "okay great and thank you both," said Devin.

"Yeah sure, you're welcome, anytime," said Celeste. "Well let us get into the kitchen with this food," and so Celeste and Jannabe headed towards the kitchen.

Within several strides Celeste and Jannabe walked into the kitchen pushing a loaded down pushcart, when suddenly Lucinda appeared in front of them saying, "oh good, you two are here," said Lucinda. "Thank you both for bringing the food and sweet treats, it's so sweet of you both."

"Yeah sure, you're welcome, and besides it's our pleasure," said Celeste. "So, where do you want all of this?"

"Come follow me and I'll show you," said Lucinda.

Within minutes Lucinda walked out through the sliding glass doors, where they saw several long tables set out with table clothes on them, "Celeste and Jannabe these are the tables we are using for the food, sweets and drinks," said Lucinda.

"Okay great," said Celeste and Jannabe, and so they started heading over to where the tables were setup.

Within several strides they walked up to the first one and started setting out the napkins, utensils, plates, bowls, cups, and two liter drinks.

Afterwards they moved onto the next table and started setting out the finger foods and platters.

Afterwards they moved onto the next table and started setting out the sweet treats.

Once they were done, they headed back towards the house, "wow

everything looks awesome out here," said Jannabe.

"Yeah, I agree, but my sister doesn't do anything halfway," said Celeste.

Jannabe smiled. "Well come on let's go put this pushcart up and then go get changed," said Celeste.

"Yes, I agree" said Jannabe. "Good, come on let's go get changed," said Celeste.

CHAPTER 11

Five thirty p.m. and Lucinda, Devin,

Dorinda, Celeste, Jannabe, Alex, Alisa, Chris and Chasity, came walking out, "oh wow, you guys look awesome," said Lucinda.

"Thanks," said the group. "Lucinda, you look amazing as a Witch," said Dorinda happily.

"Thank you," said Lucinda. "Dorinda sister, you look amazing as Elvira," said Lucinda.

"Thank you," said Dorinda. "Well now let's see what we have, and so she scanned the room and her eyes landed on Devin, "Devin you look awesome as a Warlock," Dorinda said, and then she looked at her daughters, "wow Chris you look beautiful as Cinderella."

"Thanks mom," said Chris smiling. Dorinda smiled, "yeah, you're welcome," said Chris.

She then looked at Chasity her twin

daughter saying, "wow you look beautiful as Snow White," said Dorinda.

She then looked at Celeste her baby sister who decided to dress up as Ursla, "wow baby sis you look awesome as Ursla," said Dorinda.

"Thanks, big sis," said Celeste. "Yeah, you're welcome," said Dorinda.

She looked at Jannabe who decided dress up as Belle, "oh my gosh, Jannabe you look so beautiful as Belle," said Dorinda. "Well now I can't wait to see what Elenore is dressing up as."

"Yeah, us too," said Lucinda, Devin, Celeste, Jannabe and the four girls.

"Well, when Elenore gets here I say we four sisters get together for a few minutes," said Lucinda.

Dorinda and Celeste shook their heads in agreement. Suddenly they heard the door open and heard Elenore call out, "I'm here."

A few minutes later a very pregnant Elenore walked into the den saying, "hey everyone," said Elenore.

Everyone turned around seeing that a very pregnant Elenore was standing in the room and looking like she's not feeling good, "hey Elenore, you okay?" asked Lucinda worriedly.

"Yeah and no," said Elenore. "Why do you ask?" As she was rubbing her belly and back.

"Well sis, you look like you're not feeling good," said Lucinda.

"Yeah, I'm not feeling the best but it's okay, I'm almost nine months pregnant, what do you expect," said Elenore.

"Yeah really," said Lucinda. "Well come on let us see this cute costume of yours," and so Lucinda helped her sister take her coat off, and she noticed that Elenore was dressed as Curella Deville, "omg you look amazing."

"Thank you," said Elenore smiling, all the while rubbing her belly and back.

"Yeah sure, you're welcome," said Lucinda. "Well come on let's go get you seated by the fire."

"Yeah, that'd be nice," said Elenore. "Good come on then," said Lucinda. "Oh yeah Dorinda said something about us four getting together before everyone gets here."

"Okay, that sounds like a good idea," said Elenore.

"Good." "Well come on let's go get you seated outside by the fire," said Lucinda, and so she and Elenore headed for the sliding glass doors, Lucinda pulled out her phone and text messaged Dorinda and Celeste letting them know they are needed outside a.s.a.p. and then she pressed send.

They walked out to the yard and quickly found seating, and so Elenore sat down, "sis, are you okay?" asked Lucinda. "Do you need anything?"

"Yeah, I could use a blanket," said Elenore.

"Okay, no problem," said Lucinda, and so she turned around and headed back to the house for a blanket, all the while hoping and praying that her sister was okay.

She was walking through the sliding glass doors, as Dorinda and Celeste were heading out, "hey, what's going on with Elenore?" asked Dorinda concerned.

"Well, I'm not sure, but if I have to guess she's probably in labor," said Lucinda.

"Omg, are you serious?" asked Dorinda

and Celeste.

"Yes, I'm serious," said Lucinda. "Now, will you two please get out there, while I go get a blanket and call mom and dad?"

"Yeah sure, we're heading out there now," said Dorinda and Celeste.

"Okay good," said Lucinda, and so she hurried into the house, while Dorinda and Celeste hurried out to their pregnant sister.

Lucinda grabbed the blanket, as she dialed her parent's number.

A couple of rings later her mom's voice came on the phone saying, "hello dear."

"Hey mom," said Lucinda. "So dear, what can I do for you?" her mom asked.

"Well mom, I'm wondering, are you and dad coming over for the Halloween party?" asked Lucinda.

"Yes dear, we are," said her mom. "Oh good," Lucinda said.

"Dear, is everything okay?" asked her mom.

"Yeah and no," said Lucinda. "Okay." "Well, what does that mean?" asked her mom.

"Well mom, it means I think Elenore might be in labor," said Lucinda.

"Oh lord." "Really?" said her mom. "Yes mom, I think she's in labor," said Lucinda.

"Okay." "Well, we'll be there in a little bit," said her mom.

"Okay mom, see you soon," Lucinda said.

"Okay, yeah see you soon," said her mom, and then she hung up. Lucinda couldn't help but think about her mother's coldness towards her, and her pregnant sister. It bothered her. Although her mother was never really close to any of them. Now their dad on the other hand was more closer to them.

The more she thought about her parents, the more she realized she wasn't happy about her mother coming to see her and the rest of the gang.

She was in her own little world, when she walked out to the bonfire finding her middle sister doubled over in pain, and so she hurried over saying, "hey sis, you okay?" asked Lucinda concerned.

"No, I'm not these pains are getting worse," cried Elenore.

"Oh no," said Lucinda. "So, what can I do to help?"

"I really don't know right now," said Elenore but suddenly a pain slammed into her.

"Ah, I think I'm going to call nine one-one," said Lucinda, and so she pulled out her phone and dialed nine one-one and then waited.

A couple of rings later a voice came on the line saying, "hello this is nine one-one, how may I help you?" the voice asked.

"Yes, my sister is in possible labor, and so I need an ambulance," said Lucinda.

"Okay, yes ma'am, I have an ambulance on the way," said the voice.

"Thank you," said Lucinda. "Yes ma'am, you're welcome," said the voice, and then the line went dead.

She shoved her phone in her pocket, and then she headed out the door.

As she was nearing the bonfire and her sister, the more she noticed that her sister was doubled over, and so she ran over, and bent down saying, "hey you okay sis?" asked Lucinda concerned.

"No, I'm not," said Elenore. "I'm in pain and I'm certain that this baby is trying to come on out."

"Oh no, this is not good," said Lucinda panicked. "Well, I've already called an ambulance and it's on it's way." Suddenly Lucinda's senses kicked in and she sensed something was wrong with inside her sister. In fact, it was a nagging feeling that she's had for a while. She guessed it had something to do with her unique gifts that she's had all her life, but they didn't start showing up until her teenage years.

All four sisters were given the gifts of Witchhood which were handed down from their mother and grandmother.

With the unique gifts that were handed down, each sister possesses a unique gift of her own, but they do have some of the same powers but sometimes they use them differently.

Lucinda and Dorinda are twins, and

they might possess the same powers but they each have one unique power that separates them.

"So, what can I do for you, while we wait for the ambulance to get here?" asked Lucinda.

"Well for right now just talk to me, keep my mind off this god-awful pain," said Elenore.

"Yeah sure, what do you want to talk about?" asked Lucinda curiously.

"Anything." "Everything," said Elenore. "Okay." "Well, tell me something, is this guy that you were seeing, is he the father of your unborn child, and if so, is he going to be part of you and this child's life?" Lucinda asked curiously.

"Um, well to be honest, I don't know if he's the father or not, and I don't know if he's going to be apart of me and my unborn child," said Elenore.

"Oh no, this isn't good," said Lucinda. "Well, how about you tell me everything from the beginning?"

"Well sis, I met Timmett first about a year ago and we dated off and on for a while but then things got complicated, and I just walked away," said Elenore. "Anyway, Jarrett is the latest off and on boyfriend, whom I've been with off and on for about a year now, but as of the moment, we are off and all because of his scaredness and stupidity." "So as of now I don't know who the father is of my child, but it's okay because I plan on raising this baby by myself."

Lucinda just sat there staring at her very pregnant sister with love and understanding. She now understood about the bad feelings that were plaguing her of her sisters predicament of the unknowing of who the actual father figure is of her sister's unborn child, but her instincts were telling her it's Timmett's unborn child who was mia at the moment but for now she would keep her suspicions to herself.

She quickly shifted her focus back to her sister Elenore, "wow that's crazy," said Lucinda.

"Yeah, I know," said Elenore. "Well now, I'm sorry I don't have any answers that you and I both have at the moment, but I can tell you my instincts are telling me to follow my heart and gut feelings which is to have this baby and raise him or her on my own with no regrets."

"Okay." "Well, understand where you're coming from and I'm on your side no matter what," said Lucinda.

"Thank you, sis," said Elenore. "Yeah

sure, you're welcome but I wouldn't have it any other way," said Lucinda.

Elenore smiled weakly, when suddenly she doubled over in pain, "sis, you okay?" asked Lucinda concerned.

"No, I'm not," said Elenore painfully. "This hurts bad sis."

"I'm sorry," said Lucinda concerned. "What can I do for you?"

"Nothing really, just stay with me," said Elenore.

"Yeah sure, I wouldn't have it any other way," said Lucinda caringly.

Elenore smiled weakly, "I'm so glad you're my sister," said Elenore.

Lucinda smiled, "thanks and I'm so glad to be you're my sister," said Lucinda. Suddenly Elenore and Lucinda both sensed someone was near and so they looked up and saw their mother walking up, "oh no, what's she doing here?" asked Elenore.

"Well sis, I called her," said Lucinda sheepishly. "Look sis, I thought it would be nice to include her, but I'm rethinking my decision."

"Okay, I understand," said Elenore. Suddenly they heard, "hey girls."

Both Elenore and Lucinda looked up and saw their mother, "hi mother," said both girls.

"So girls, what's going on?" asked their mother.

"Nothing really," said the girls. "Oh really," said their mother. "Well somethings going on." "I can feel it." "Girls don't forget I have powers of my own and I my senses are telling me something is wrong, now tell me, what's going on here?"

"Well mom, I'm over eight months pregnant and I'm possibly in labor," said

Elenore hatefully.

"Oh my." "Well, that's interesting," said her mom. "Well, why didn't I know any of this?"

"Well mom, to be honest you've never really been apart of any of us girls and so I kinda figured you wouldn't care anything about me and my pregnancy," said Elenore bluntly.

Their mom just stood there stunned, she couldn't believe that bother her girls were being the way they were, and that her middle child was due any day to have her baby.

The more she thought about what her middle child had said, the more she realized that she hadn't been the type of mother they needed, and at that moment she started chastising herself for the horrible mothering she had done. It was downright despicable. She was horrified at herself for how she has been towards her four girls.

Her thoughts came back to the present, and she just stared at her two girls, and then said, "girls I owe you an apology for being a horrible parent and mother," said their mom tearfully.

Her two girls just stared at her for a few minutes, they didn't know what to say, so they just stayed quiet contemplating on what to say to her, and then both girls said, "thanks mom for the apology," said Elenore and Lucinda.

"Yeah, you're welcome girls," said their mom. "So girls, what can I do to help?"

"Well mom, you could help with the party," said Lucinda.

"Yeah sure, anything to help out," said her mom.

Suddenly they heard the voices of the

guests coming through the air, "oh great, our guests are starting to come in," said Lucinda.

Suddenly they heard a blood curdling scream come from Elenore, as she was holding her belly and back, "omg, this is bad pains," said Elenore painfully. "Man, I believe this baby is trying to come now."

"Omg." "Seriously?" said her mom. "Yes seriously," said Elenore.

"Omg." "Well, what do I need to do?" her mom asked.

"Mom, just help with the Halloween party," said Lucinda.

"Okay dear, I'm on it," said her mom, and then she headed out to greet the guests.

When she was out of earshot, "wow I can't believe it mom actually apologized," said Elenore.

"Yeah, me either," said Lucinda. "Sis, I wasn't really expecting it either."

"Yeah, no doubt, me either," said Elenore. "Mother's apology came out of nowhere."

"Yeah really," said Lucinda. "Well anyway, I'm not sure how to take it."

"Me either," said Elenore. Suddenly Elenore doubled over and then the next thing she knew she felt wetness and looked down and her clothes were wet, "uh sis, I think we have a problem," said Elenore.

"Oh yeah, what kinda problem?" asked Lucinda curiously.

"Well look down," said Elenore, and so both Elenore and Lucinda looked down and immediately noticed Elenore's clothes were wet. "Omg, this is crazy," said Lucinda. "I believe your water just broke."

"Yeah, I believe you're right, but I also

believe this baby is on it's way out now," said Elenore.

"Omg seriously?" said Lucinda. "Yes seriously," said Elenore.

"Omg." "So, why do you say this?" asked Lucinda.

"Well for starters I feel pressure and it's making me want to push," said Elenore painfully.

"Okay." "Well, what do we need to do?" asked Lucinda.

"Well go ahead and get that blanket ready incase we need it," Elenore said.

"Okay," said Lucinda, and so she picked up the blanket. "Okay, here it is."

"Great," said Elenore. Suddenly she let out a scream, and then said, "omg here comes another horrible pain," said Elenore.

"Oh wow, that sounds bad," said Lucinda.

"Yeah, well it doesn't feel too good," said Elenore,

"I'm sure it doesn't," said Lucinda. "Anyway, what can I do?"

"No not really, just stay close," said Elenore, but suddenly another pain slammed into her forcefully. "Omg, that was a bad one." But before she could say anything else another pain slammed into her but more forcefully, "omg," said Elenore.

"Yeah, that one was close," said Lucinda.

"Yeah, no doubt, too close," said Elenore. "You know Sis, I think this baby might be here before we know it."

"Yeah, I know, it looks like it," said Lucinda. "Well maybe you'll have this baby tonight."

"Yeah maybe, I hope so anyway," said

Elenore. "I hope in the next hour or so."

"Yeah, that would be nice," Lucinda said.

"Yeah, it would be, I'm nine months pregnant, and I'm ready for this baby to be here," said Elenore. Suddenly another pain slammed into her and then suddenly she felt pressure, "omg, I think this is it."

"You do," said Lucinda. "Yeah, I do," said Elenore.

"Are you sure?" asked Lucinda cautiously.

"Yes, I'm sure," Elenore said. "But I'm telling you something doesn't feel right."

"Oh yeah." "What do you mean?" Lucinda asked curiously.

"Well, I mean is something feels strange inside, and I can't explain it," said Elenore.

"Oh really?" "Well try me," Lucinda

said.

"Okay." "Well sis, it almost feels like I have two in my belly," Elenore said.

"Omg." "Are you serious?" Lucinda asked curiously.

"Yes, I'm serious," said Elenore. "Omg." "That's crazy," said Lucinda.

"Yeah, no doubt, but my gut feelings are always right," Elenore said.

"Okay then." "Well, I know all about them gut feelings and yes your gut never is wrong," Lucinda said. "In fact, the universe gives us many non-material things such as choices, chances and intuition."

Suddenly Elenore doubled over with another pain slamming into her, and then she looked up saying, "uh I think this is it," said Elenore.

"Omg." "Really?" "Seriously?" said Lucinda.

"Yes, I'm serious," Elenore said, and then suddenly Elenore doubled over in pain, "omg this hurts."

"Yeah, I bet," said Lucinda. "So, what can I do to help?"

"Well, you can bring that blanket and squat down in front of me placing the blanket underneath me," Elenore said.

"Yeah sure, anything to help," said Lucinda, and so she grabbed the blanket and quickly moved over and squatted down in front of her sister, "okay, I'm ready, when you are," said Lucinda.

"Okay good," said Elenore smiling weakly, and then suddenly another pain slammed into her and then suddenly she felt something give, "omg, I think it's coming."

"Seriously?" said Lucinda. "Yes seriously," Elenore said painfully.

"Okay, well I'm ready, when you are," said Lucinda.

Elenore smiled weakly, "okay, well here goes nothing," said Elenore.

A few minutes later they had a baby boy laying in Lucinda's arms, "omg, he's so beautiful," gushed Lucinda.

"Thank you, and yes he is," said Elenore tearfully, but suddenly she doubled over again with a severe pain, and then the next thing she knew another baby came out into Lucinda's arms, "omg, we have a little girl," gushed Lucinda.

Elenore smiled tearfully, "thank you, I think so," said Elenore.

"Well, how about we get them dried off and then introduce them to the family," said Lucinda.

"Okay, yeah that would be nice," said Elenore smiled.

"Okay good," said Lucinda, and so Lucinda and Elenore quickly wiped off the two newborns and then wrapped them, "hey sis, can you go get everyone for me?" asked Elenore.

"Yeah sure, no problem," said Lucinda "Why though?"

"Well to be honest, I don't feel stable enough to stand up and walk," said Elenore.

"Oh okay, I understand completely," Lucinda said, and then she stood up and handed the babies to Elenore, "here you go mommy," said Lucinda.

"Thank you," said Elenore smiling. "Yeah sure, no problem, and you're welcome," said Lucinda, and then she headed off in the direction of the family.

When Lucinda was out of sight, Elenore just sat there and let the tears fall, she was so mad at herself for running off two men, who she clearly enjoyed being with, but she found something wrong with them and she let them go. Well, more less she ran them off, and now she was totally alone raising twins, and suddenly the tears came harder.

She was in her own little world, when she suddenly heard voices, and so she quickly came back to earth and started calming herself down.

A few minutes later she was swarmed with family and friends congratulating her and pouring love and support on her and her twins.

After several minutes had gone by, the family and friends started backing away.

Once she wasn't smothered anymore, she sensed her mother close, and so she took a couple of deep calming breaths, and then said, "hey mother." "What do you want?"

"Well dear, I wanted to come over and check on you and meet my new grandbabies," said her mother.

"Oh really?" said Elenore. "Yes really," said her mother.

"Well mother, I don't believe you," Elenore said.

Helen her mother stayed quiet for a few minutes, she didn't know how to respond to her daughter's response to her trying to show love and support.

The more she thought about it, the more she realized that it was her fault the reason her daughter Elenore was being the way she was, and at that moment she knew what she had to do and so she took a couple of deep calming breaths and then bent down looking into her daughter's eyes and then said, "Elenore dear, I'm sorry for everything, and I want to make things right with you and your sisters," said Helen.

Elenore just stared at her mother, she couldn't believe that her mother was actually apologizing for the way she's been all her life, and her sister's lives. They'd been waiting and hoping forever for her to apologize to them and become an actual mother.

The more she thought about her mother and her horrible ways, the more she realized that the woman who she called mother was actually trying to be apart of her family. She smiled tearfully.

After a few minutes she looked at her mother saying, "thank you for the apology," said Elenore. "That means the world to me."

Helen smiled tearfully, "you're welcome, but I owe you so much more than just an apology," said Helen. "Anyway, I promise, I'm going to do my best to do everything in my power to get back in with you Elenore and your sisters."

Elenore smiled tearfully, she longed to hear those words so long along that her mother spoke now, and it made her feel good but deep down she wondered why now. What changed?

The more she thought about her mother and her words, the more she thought that just maybe her mother was actually trying to be better and do better. Well anyway that's what she's hoping for anyway.

A few minutes later she broke away from her thoughts, and looked at her mother saying, "thanks mom, that really means a lot to me, and I would love to have you in mine and my newborn babies lives," said Elenore.

Helen smiled tearfully, "thank you, and I would love to get to know you and your newborn babies," said Helen happily.

Elenore smiled, and then said, "well now come meet your grandson and granddaughter," said Elenore.

Helen smiled, and then said, "yes, I would love to meet my newborn twins," said Helen.

"Well come on then, come meet your newborn grandbabies," said Elenore happily.

Helen smiled tearfully, she was scared and excited at the same time, and so walked up and in front of her daughter and the tears started sliding down her cheeks, her daughter and newborn grandbabies were just a vision of beautifulness, and suddenly a feeling of true love for her daughter and her twins was so strong,

strong then it ever had been. "Oh honey, they are beautiful," gushed Helen.

"Thanks mom," said Elenore tearfully. "So honey, what have named these sweet babies of yours anyway?" asked Helen.

"Well mom to be honest I haven't named them yet," said Elenore. Suddenly they heard sirens coming their way. "Oh good, the ambulance is finally here."

"Yes, that's a good thing, and if you don't mind, I would like to ride with you and my grandbabies," said Helen.

"Oh wow, yes I would love for you to be with us," said Elenore,

"Good, I'm glad," said Helen. Suddenly the paramedics were walking up, "hi we're looking for a Miss Lamberson," the first man said.

"Yes sir, I'm Miss Lamberson," said Elenore.

"Great." "Well let us get these two babies from you," said the man, man so he had two women came up and introduce themselves and then each took a baby and quickly wrapped them in a blanket.

As the two women took the babies with them, the paramedic man came and helped her into a wheelchair and then the paramedic and her mom walked over to the ambulance and soon after they had Elenore on a gurney and the babies in incubators and her mom sitting in the front seat and they were on their way to the hospital.

CHAPTER 12

Fifteen minutes later the ambulance pulled into the hospital parking lot and pulled around to the ER side, and soon after they were unloading Elenore and her babies.

As the paramedics were handling her daughter and the babies, she pulled out her phone and tapped the screen and found her daughter Lucinda's number and so she clicked on it and quickly typed out I'm at the Dublin General Hospital with Elenore and her twins, and then she pressed send.

CHAPTER 13

Lucinda was talking amongst family and friends when she heard her phone buzz and so she pulled it out and tapped the screen and saw that the message was from her mother letting her know that she was at the hospital with Elenore and her babies, she smiled happily, she was glad that their mother was with their sister and her newborn twins. Her call out to the universe came through and they answered her call out for help.

She was superstitious of everything and that's why she had everything known to man in remedies for everything from sickness to heartache. In fact, all the women and her dad were superstitious, and they believed in the natural remedies of the world and universe.

She broke her thinking process, and looked at the group of family and friends and said, "hey everyone I have some news for you," said Lucinda.

The group quickly started calming down.

Once everyone was quiet, Lucinda looked at the group, and then said, "hey everyone about thirty minutes or so ago I helped my sister Elenore deliver her twin newborn babies," said Elenore.

Everyone was quiet, quiet enough that you could hear a pin drop.

A few minutes went by and then suddenly clapping, cheers, whistles and congratulations came from the group, and at that moment she felt the love and support of her family and friends surround her. She breathed in the love and support and let it engulf her and seep through her body and soul. It was wonderful having family and friends surrounding her and showing her their love and support for her and everyone around her.

She came back to earth, "well everyone, thank you for the love and support that you've showed towards me and my family, but I'm sorry to say we need to cut this party short so me and my sisters Dorinda and Celeste can go see our sister Elenore and her newborn babies," said

Lucinda. Suddenly Dorinda and Celeste appeared in front of her saying, "wow sis that's amazing that you were there to witness Elenore's newborn babies being born," said Dorinda.

"Thank you, sis, but I wouldn't have it any other way," said Lucinda. "Oh, and by the way I think mother is trying to get back in with us, so just a heads up she's with Elenore and her babies at the hospital."

Dorinda and Celeste just stood there stock still, they couldn't believe what they were hearing, their mother actually with one of them acting like a mother for once in their lives. "Wow that's unbelievable," said Dorinda. "She has some nerve."

"Yeah, no doubt," said Celeste. "She's got some nerve."

"Yeah, I know she's never been there for us, but I still think we need to give her a chance for those babies sake and our kids sakes," said Lucinda. "Look I know it's not going to be easy or overnight, but we need to try and include her and hopefully she will change into the mother we all need and deserve."

Dorinda and Celeste shook their heads in agreement, "okay we'll give her a chance," said Dorinda.

Lucinda smiled, "good, well come on let's go meet these newborn babies," said Lucinda.

"Yes we're ready to meet these two newborns, and of course Elenore," said Dorinda and Celeste.

"We are her support group after all," said Dorinda." "She doesn't have no man in her life that's worth keeping."

"Yeah true, you're right on all accounts," said Lucinda. "Well come on let's go.”

CHAPTER 14

Fifteen minutes later Lucinda pulled into the parking lot of Dublin General and soon after they were hurrying inside.

Lucinda, Dorinda and Celeste walked up to the nurse's station, “yes ma'am, how may I help you?” asked the lady.

“Yes ma'am, my sister Elenore Lamberson and her twin newborns were brought here a little while ago,” said Lucinda.

“Okay, yes ma'am, let me look and see where she is for you,” said the lady.

“Okay, thank you, that would be nice,” said Lucinda.

“Yeah sure, no problem,” said the lady, and so the lady tapped a few keys, and then said, "okay, Ms. Lamberson is on the maternity ward which is on the third floor."

Lucinda smiled, "thank you ma'am," said Lucinda, and so Lucinda, Dorinda and Celeste headed towards the elevators.

Within several strides they walked up to the elevators and stepped on and Lucinda pushed three on the panel.

As the sisters rode the elevator up to three, they chatted about everything.

A few minutes later the elevator stopped on three and the doors slid open and the three sisters walked off the elevator heading towards the nurse's station.

Lucinda, Dorinda and Celeste walked up to the nurse's station, "yes ladies, how may I help you?" asked the male nurse.

"Yes sir, we are looking for our sister Ms. Elenore Lamberson," said Lucinda.

"Alright, well let me check and see where she is," said the male nurse, and so he tapped a few keys, and then said, "alright ladies, your sister is in room one twenty-five."

"Okay great, and thanks," said Lucinda, Dorinda and Celeste, and then they headed down the hall.

Within several strides Lucinda and her two sisters walked up to the door of their sister's room, "well this is it, let's go meet our newest nephew and niece, and of course see our mother," said Lucinda.

Dorinda and Celeste smiled, and shook their heads in agreement, and so Lucinda knocked, and waited.

A minute or two went by and then the door opened up and there stood their mother Helen, "hey girls," said Helen.

"Hey mother," said Lucinda, Dorinda

and Celeste.

"Well come on in, come on and meet your new nephew and niece," said Helen, and so Helen moved out of the way for her girls to walk through the door.

As Helen was shutting the door back, Lucinda, Dorinda and Celeste walked over to their sister Elenore's bed, "hey sis," they said.

Elenore smiled, "you three came," she squealed.

"Yeah, why wouldn't we?" asked Lucinda.

Elenore smiled, "well I'm glad you three came," said Elenore.

"Yeah, we are too," said Lucinda. "Well come see my new babies," said Elenore.

Lucinda smiled, "yeah sure, we would love too," said Lucinda, and so she and her two sisters walked over and looked at the two babies, "oh wow, they are beautiful," gushed Lucinda, Dorinda and Celeste.

"Thank you," said Elenore happily. Lucinda, Dorinda and Celeste smiled.

"Well sis, what did you name these two?" asked Lucinda.

"Well to be honest I haven't yet," Elenore said.

"Okay, but why though?" asked Lucinda curiously.

"Well to be honest, I wanted to see if one of the two guys shows up and owns up to fatherhood, but they haven't yet, so therefore I'm getting ready to name them," said Elenore.

"Okay, we understand that," her three sisters said.

Elenore smiled, "good and thank you," said Elenore.

"Well now, tell me, what are you

thinking for the boys names?" asked Lucinda.

"Well sis, I've made a list of boys names, but I'm leaning towards one though," said Elenore.

"Okay, so what is it?" asked Lucinda curiously.

"Liam Michael is my chosen boys name," said Elenore happily.

"Oh wow, that's a beautiful name choice," said Lucinda, Dorinda and Celeste.

"Thank you, I think so," Elenore said happily.

"Yeah sure, you're welcome," said the three. "Well now, what are you going to name this little girl?"

"Well, I have a list of girls names but I'm leaning towards one," said Elenore.

"Okay great, so what is it?" asked Lucinda.

Well, I've chosen Ivey Marie for my daughter's name," said Elenore.

"Oh wow, that's a beautiful name for a little girl," said Lucinda, Dorinda and Celeste.

"Thank you, I think so," said Elenore happily.

"Yeah sure, you're welcome," said Lucinda, Dorinda and Celeste.

"Well now, how about we share the baby naming with our mother?" said Lucinda.

"Okay." "Yeah, that would be nice," said Elenore, with Dorinda and Celeste shaking their heads reluctantly.

Lucinda smiled, "okay, well then it's settled then," said Lucinda, and so she turned around and said, "hey mom."

"Yes Lucinda," said Helen. "Mom, come over her and be apart of this moment,

Elenore has finally figured out the baby names for these two," said Lucinda.

"Okay but are you sure you four really want me over there?" asked Helen nervously.

"Yes, Mother it's fine, so come on let's go visit," said Lucinda.

Helen smiled weakly, she still wasn't sure how welcome she would be considering how awful she's been toward her girls all these years. It hurt her down deep to the bone that she was that awful mother throughout her girls growing up years. She chastised herself over and over for what she had put her girls through their growing up years.

She was in her own little world, when her thoughts were interrupted by the sound of her daughter calling her name, and so she came back to earth, "yes honey," said

Helen.

"Mom, come on let's go visit with Elenore, Celeste and Dorinda and the new babies," said Lucinda.

"Okay, yeah I'm ready to meet them," said Helen. "By the way, what did she name the babies anyway?"

"Well Mother she named her baby boy Liam Michael and she named her baby girl Ivey Jane," said Lucinda happily.

"Oh wow, she chose cute names for them babies," said Helen happily.

"Yes ma'am, she did," said Lucinda smiling. "Well come on let's go see these new babies and Elenore."

Helen smiled weakly, "yes I'm ready," said Helen.

"Great," said Lucinda, and so Lucinda, her mother and Dorinda and Celeste walked over to Elenore's bed, "wow Elenore honey these babies are beautiful and their chosen names are very cute," said Helen.

"Thanks, that means a lot coming from you mother," said Elenore.

"Yeah sure, but it's the truth and to be honest I owe you and your sisters many apologizes for how I've been toward you four all your lives, it was so wrong of me to treat you four so badly all through your growing up years." "Girls I'm so sorry for being such a horrible mother towards you four, but I promise now that I'm going to be a better mother towards you four girls and your children," said Helen tearfully.

Lucinda, Dorinda, Elenore and Celeste stood stock still, they couldn't believe what they were hearing from their mother. It was crazy but all they could do was hope and pray that she was being honest with them and herself, but time would tell and not to mention that the universe would be watching over them.

"Thank you, Mother for the kind words," said Lucinda, Dorinda, Elenore and Celeste.

"Yeah sure, but it's the truth," said Helen. "I'm telling girls everything I said I meant." "So please forgive me and give me a chance."

"Okay, we forgive you, but we're not promising anything, but we'll try and give you a chance," said Lucinda, Dorinda, Elenore and Celeste.

"Okay, thank you for the forgiveness and yes I understand why you're skittish on giving me a chance, but please all I'm asking is try and give me a chance," said Helen. "Now girls I have to tell you that I've been in contact with the elders, and it's been an awaking experience but a truthful one at that."

"Um." "Okay." "Well, that's quite interesting to know," said Lucinda. "So, tell us, why have you been in close contact with the elders?"

"Well girls, it's been brought to my attention that we've got some unwanted visitors coming our way and it's troublesome," said Helen.

"Oh really?" said Lucinda curiously. "What kinda visitors are heading this way?"

"Honey, I don't know really, all I know is we need to be ready for anything from here on out," said Helen.

"Okay." "Well, whatever this is we need to stay focused and alert at all times," said Lucinda.

"Yes ma'am, we agree," said Lucinda, Dorinda, Elenore and Celeste."

"Girls, I can't tell you how much I love

you four and my grandchildren and I'm so thankful that you girls are forgiving towards me, and I hope sometime soon you will give me a chance to prove to you that I can and want to be apart of this family of mine," said Helen.

"Mom, we love you too, and yes we do forgive you, but you have to understand that it's going to take time for us to let you back into our family fold," said Lucinda, Dorinda, Elenore and Celeste tearfully.

"Oh girls, thank you for the love, support, honesty and forgiveness, and the chance of family and happiness that I threw away everything for proudness so long ago," said Helen heartbrokenly.

"Oh mom, you're more then welcome, and yes you're part of this family no doubt, and always have been," said Lucinda, Dorinda, Elenore and Celeste sweetly.

Helen smiled brightly, "well now it looks like you Elenore got your wish of having these twins on your favorite Holiday Halloween," said Helen.

"Yes mom, you're right I did get my wish, and I'm so happy and grateful," said Elenore weakly.

Helen smiled, she was happy and proud of her third daughter and her newborn babies. It did her heart good to be apart of this very special time. Now she had to see about her youngest daughter Celeste and her oldest daughter Dorinda. Anyway, it's been brought to her attention that her oldest daughter Dorinda is going through a rough time with her marriage. Her husband Demitre isn't a good man. In fact, from what I'm being told is that he is very abusive in all ways and the universe and elders are not happy about the situation and they are making it my business. All though my oldest daughter is very private person and therefore she doesn't speak about any of her problems relating to her marriage or husband. Anyway, the elders and universe have asked me to step in and see what I can do to fix this situation of hers and so that's what I'm starting to work on.

Now onto my youngest daughter Celeste, she is super independent, a very much a loner, and a workaholic, and so she doesn't have much time for herself or relationships, and so that's where I come in. Although, I've never really been in my four girls lives physically, I've always been in their lives mentally and spiritually guiding them throughout their growing up years but somewhere along the way a couple of them lost their way and ended up on different paths.

Now onto her middle child Elenore, Elenore is her vivacious, loving, spontaneous and independent child, who is singly raising her newborn twins, and whom she has no idea who their father figure is, and that's where I come in.

Now onto my oldest daughter Lucinda, Lucinda is the most together woman that I've ever seen, she has everything together in her life, she has an amazing husband and two wonderful children, and she also co-owns and operates a business of her own with her twin sister, so I have no worries with this one as of right now, but there are no guaranties.

She was lost in her thoughts, when she suddenly heard her name being called and so she slowly floated back to earth and answered, "yes."

"Mom, where did you go?" asked

Lucinda.

"Oh, nowhere really just in my thoughts," said Helen.

"Uh huh." "Okay, we understand that," said Lucinda.

Helen smiled. "Well now, how about we get visiting?" Helen said.

CHAPTER 15

November third two thousand and twenty fourteen, Monday afternoon around three forty-five and Elenore and her newborn babies were just discharged from Dublin General Hospital, when she heard a voice say, "excuse me ma'am."

Elenore turned around seeing a man standing near, "yes sir," said Elenore. "What can I do for you?"

"Well ma'am, I was seeing if you had a

ride," said the man.

"Ah, yes I have a ride," said Elenore. "I called a cab."

"Oh good, that's good to hear," said the man. "Well then I need to be going," and so he turned around and started walking away, when he suddenly stopped and turned around saying, "by the way I'm Trevor Roberston," he said.

"Okay." "Well, I'm Elenore Lamberson," said Elenore.

"Alright, well it's nice to meet you ma'am," he said.

"Yeah, and it's nice to meet you too," said Trevor smiling, and then he turned around and walked away.

When he was out of sight, Elenore smiled to herself, wow, he was on the cute side, and he seemed nice enough. Although she wasn't actively looking for anyone or anything at the moment, but it was still fun to look at the opposite sex.

The more she thought about the man Trevor Roberston, the more she realized she was intrigued about him and so she made a mental note to look him up later.

She was in her own little world, when she was interrupted by someone calling for her, and so she slowly came back to earth and answered, "yes."

"Ah, yes ma'am your ride is here," said the woman.

"Thank you," said Elenore. Yes ma'am, you're welcome." "Well here let me help you out to your waiting cab," said the woman.

"Thank you, that would be great," said Elenore.

"Yeah sure, you're welcome but I don't mind," said the woman, and so she stepped out from behind the desk and walked over and grabbed ahold of the wheelchair handles and then started pushing the wheelchair towards the sliding glass doors.

A couple of minutes later she and her babies were being helped into the waiting cab.

Once she and her babies and all their things were safely inside, the cab driver, asked, "where too ma'am?"

Elenore rattled off her address to him, and then he typed it into the navigator and then said, "okay well let's get you three home," he said.

"Yes please," said Elenore. "I'm ready." The man smiled.

As she was enjoying the ride, she got thinking about her mom and her sisters and the reason none of them could come pick her and her babies up from the hospital, which didn't make any since, but whatever she would find her own way home, no big deal.

The more she thought about her sisters and her mother and their crazy reasoning of being busy with things that had to be done today, the more it perturbed her, and to think that she actually thought that they would be overly happy to help her but oh no they chose to do their own thing. Well anyway she didn't need their help, she could do everything on her own.

She smiled to herself, she was excited about being home with her new babies. Although it was going to be different with it just being her by herself.

CHAPTER 16

After, a fifteen minute ride, the cab

pulled into her driveway, where she noticed half a dozen cars lined in front of her home, "wow what is going on here?" she mumbled.

"Well ma'am, I'm not sure but it looks like you're having some kinda get together," he said.

"Yes, it looks that way," said Elenore. "Well anyway let me get everything out," and so she opened the door and stepped out and she walked around to the back finding the man-driver had beat her to it and he had the trunk open, and he was already unloading her things, "wow you're fast," said Elenore.

"Yes ma'am, I kinda have to be with this job," the man said, not noticing who he was talking to at the moment.

As he was lifting out the last bag, he looked up seeing the lady from the hospital earlier and it didn't hit him until now that she was the same lady that he'd picked up at the hospital, "wow this is crazy." "I saw you earlier with your newborns at the Dublin General Hospital and I guess from there I became your cab driver unexpectedly," said Trevor.

She looked at him strangely, and then suddenly it hit her that he was the same guy that she saw at the hospital, "omg." "Wow." "Okay this is crazy," said Elenore. "Well Mister, it's nice to see you again."

"Um, first my name is Trevor Roberston, and yes it's nice to see you again young lady," he said.

Elenore smiled, she couldn't believe in a million years that this would happen to her, her meeting someone, but then again she was happy it did because he was really cute, and he seemed to be really nice.

She was lost in her own thoughts, when she was interrupted by someone calling her name, and so she came back to earth saying, "yes."

"Well come on let's get these two babies out of the car and into that house," said Trevor.

"Yeah, I agree," said Elenore, and so she reached in a unbuckled a baby, while Trevor reached in and unbuckled the other baby.

Once they had the babies out of the car, they shut the car doors, and then started down the driveway heading towards the steps, when suddenly the door flew open and her sister Lucinda walked out onto the porch saying, "yay you're finally here," gushed Lucinda.

Elenore smiled, "yes we're finally home," said Elenore happily.

Lucinda smiled, and then she came running down the steps, and up to the guy saying, "here let me take that baby carrier off your hands," said Lucinda.

"Thanks, and yes here you go," said Trevor.

"Thanks," said Lucinda, and then she carefully took the baby carrier from the man.

"Well now, I'll go get the other stuff, while you two ladies take these babies inside," said Trevor.

"Okay great, and thanks," said Elenore and Lucinda sweetly.

"Yeah sure, no problem," Trevor said, and then he headed back to the cab.

On his way back to his cab, he couldn't get the beautiful dark headed lady out of his head, and at that moment he knew he wanted to get to know her better.

The more he thought about the young lady, the more intrigued he became.

He broke his thoughts, and quickly rounded the cab and grabbed ahold of the pushcart and started heading back towards the steps.

As he was nearing, the beautiful young lady appeared on the porch saying, "thank you for bringing my stuff to me," said Elenore happily.

"Yeah sure, you're welcome, but I don't mind," said Trevor happily.

Elenore smiled, "thank you for being sweet," said Elenore.

Trevor smiled, he liked her, she was really sweet and beautiful, and he wanted to get to know her through and through, and he planned on doing just that.

"Well young lady, I have to be going for now, but do you think I could get your number?" he said.

Elenore stared at him for a few minutes, and then she said, "okay sure," said Elenore, and then she rattled off her number.

Trevor smiled, "thank you, young lady," said Trevor. "I'll be in touch soon," and then he walked away.

When he was gone, she smiled to herself, wow he's really nice, and really cute.

The more she thought about the very handsome Trevor Roberston, the more she realized she wanted to get to know him more. In fact, he intrigued her. She smiled to herself, the man Trevor Roberston intrigued her to no end.

She was in her own little world, when suddenly her thoughts were interrupted by someone calling her name, and so she slowly crept back to earth saying, "yeah," said Elenore.

"Come on sis let's get this stuff inside," said Lucinda.

Elenore smiled, "yes let's," said Elenore, and so Elenore and Lucinda carried the pushcart up the steps and onto the porch and then heading through the door, as the cab was leaving the driveway.

As they were walking through the door, when suddenly she was surprised with people scattered everywhere, "wow, what is all this?" said Elenore curiously.

"Well sis, we wanted to do something special for you, and so mom suggested we do a baby shower for you," said Lucinda.

"Oh wow, this is awesome and so sweet of you, thank you so much, this is such a big help," gushed Elenore tearfully. "Now if I just had someone here to stay with me to help for a month or so for me to get used to being a mom."

Lucinda discreetly looked at her mom, and her mom discreetly looked back at her and smiled.

Elenore looked around the room full of family and friends, and she smiled, she was so grateful for all the love and support, and then suddenly her eyes landed on her mother, and so she walked over and wrapped her arms around her mother saying, "thank you mom for everything," Elenore gushed.

"Yes honey, you're welcome but I wanted to be apart of this special occasion of yours," said Helen.

"Omg, thank you so much for this perfect surprise," said Elenore tearfully.

Helen smiled tearfully, "oh baby you're more then welcome but in my opinion, I owe you this and so much more, and so that's why I've decided that I'm going to stay here with you for as long as you need giving you all the help and support you could ever want or need," said Helen tearfully.

"Oh mom, that's awesome news and thank you so much," said Elenore.

"Yes baby, you're welcome, and I'm glad to be here and apart of this wonderful and blissful time," said Helen.

Elenore smiled. "Mom." "Yes baby," said Helen.

"Mom, later on after this shower is over and everyone is gone, I want to talk to you about something," said Elenore.

"Okay, I see," said Helen. "Well, does this something have a name?"

"Um, wow." "How did you know?" asked Elenore curiously.

"Well let's just call it mother's intuition right now, and then later I'll explain," Helen said.

"Okay mom, we'll leave it at that for now," Elenore said.

"Okay good," said Helen. "Well now let's get this baby shower underway, shall we?"

Elenore smiled, "yeah let's get in there," said Elenore happily, and so Helen, Elenore and Lucinda walked inside to the over filled room of people, presents and foods.

CHAPTER 17

Eight o'clock rolled around, and the baby-shower was over, and the guests were leaving.

Once everyone was gone, Helen,

Elenore, Lucinda, Dorinda, Celeste and Jennabe were in the kitchen, "wow this was a wonderful baby-shower," said Elenore. "I think I got everything I'm ever going to need or want."

"Yes sis, I believe you did," said Lucinda.

Elenore smiled, "thank you ladies for everything, this means the world to me," gushed Elenore.

"Yeah sure, you're more than welcome, but you deserve this and more," said Helen, Lucinda, Dorinda and Celeste lovingly. "Now, how about you tell us about this cute cab driver from yesterday?"

"Well, there's really not much to tell," said Elenore.

"Uh huh." "Well, I don't believe that," said Helen. "So, spill already."

"Okay." Well, all I know is his name is

Trevor Roberston and he drives a cab," said Elenore nonchalantly.

"Uh huh." "That's all she says," said Helen.

"Yeah, well that's all there is," said Elenore. "Although he did ask for my number and I kinda gave it to men."

"Oh wow, and you said there's not much to tell," said Helen.

"Yeah, well I'm not going to hold my breath, I have two newborn babies to care for, so therefore I don't see any man wanting to be with me seeing that I'm a single new mom," said Elenore.

"Okay honey, I understand your feelings, but don't let the fear of loneliness and let downs of people and things control you and lead you," said Helen.

Elenore stared at her mom tearfully, and then said, "thank you mom," said

Elenore.

"Yeah sure, dear but I'm telling you the universe has a plan for you and your babies, you just have to be patient and the right person will come into your life soon, that's all I'm saying," said Helen. "Look you just have to trust in the universe and yourself to know when the right person is right front of you."

"Okay mom, I'm hearing you and I'll try and be open minded but I'm telling you mom there is no man in his right man is ever going to be with a single woman who just happens to be a single mom of newborn twins," said Elenore.

"Okay, I see," said Helen. "Well honey, just give up on love and happiness, and certainly don't worry about anything because the universe has it under control."

Elenore smiled at her mom, and then

said, "mom I promise I'll try and be open minded to the unique possibilities," said Elenore.

"Okay, well that's all I'm asking," said Helen.

Elenore smiled, "okay then," said Elenore.

"Girls, I know I haven't been here in physical form for you four girls throughout your growing up years but I've been here with you mentally and spiritually helping and guiding you through the universes control system and which I've seen everything each of you have been through and going through and I'm here to tell you I'm here to help and give you guidance.

"Hum." "Okay." "Well, that's interesting to know," said the four.

"What do you mean?" Helen asked curiously.

"What do we mean?" asked the four. "Mom, you've always been the type of woman who believes in the supernatural world and the uniqueness of it," said Lucinda.

"Yes, you're right, I've always been in tune with the supernatural world and all it's uniqueness but girls it's the world we live in and we have to be open to new possibilities," said Helen.

"Okay mom, we get it, and we understand what you're trying to tell us," said Lucinda.

"Okay good, I'm glad," said Helen. "Now, listen girls, I can tell you all four of you each have something special inside of you but it's up to you to figure it out." "You have so many new possibilities heading your way in all categories, you just have to be patient, and everything will come to you in due time."

All four girls just stared at their mother in shock, they couldn't believe what they'd just heard, but then again they could because she was a Witch through, and through, and her abilities to read people, to read into situations, and other things were of true value.

"Mom, you're right and we promise to try and have an open mind and heart to new opportunities of all origins of life," said Lucinda, with her three sisters shaking their heads in agreement.

"Good, I'm glad, that makes me really happy," said Helen. "Girls, I'm so grateful and happy and relieved to be back in your lives now and forever."

Her four daughters smiled at her with open minds, hearts and souls, and at that moment she walked right into their waiting loving arms.

After a few minutes they pulled apart, "wow now, welcome home mom," said her four girls.

"Thank you, girls it feels good to be back home with you four," said Helen. "But you know what's funny, all the time I thought I was being shoved in the direction of helping you four girls, but instead it turns out that this old Witch mom needed a wake-up call from my demon minded heart, so thank you for rescuing me from myself."

Lucinda, Dorinda, Elenore and Celeste smiled, "you're welcome, we think," said her four girls.

"Well come on girls, let's get visiting and get to knowing each other again," Helen said, and so Helen and her four girls headed outside to the firepit for some much catching up.

The End

www.ingramcontent.com/pod-product-compliance
Lightning Source LLC
Chambersburg PA
CBHW072108150726
47999CB00005B/1941